STEM-LAND

The Noble Gases Come to the Rescue

By: Ashley McAlpin

Ashley McAlpin

Dedicated to the village of family, friends, educators,
and strangers that helped me along the way.

CHAPTER 1

ELEPHANT TOOTHPASTE

Purple foam burst into the air like toothpaste out of a fresh tube.

Ms. Detore's 3rd grade class screeched and clapped.

In the front row sat a girl with a thousand curls. Her hands were slapped against her cheeks. She could not believe what she had seen.

"How did you do that?" she exclaimed.

Ms. Detore smiled then said, "Science Mitry!"

Science! Mitry was impressed. This was her first science class and it was already off to a good start.

Ms. Detore clapped her hands twice to get the class' attention. "Class, what you just saw was Elephant Toothpaste."

Elephant toothpaste!

Mitry looked at the giant squiggles of foam. It certainly looked like there was enough to brush an elephant's teeth, maybe even a herd of elephants' teeth.

"Just because we call it toothpaste doesn't mean you want to put it in your mouth or an elephant's." Continued Ms. Detore.

She pointed to the ingredients on her demonstration table.

"Elephant toothpaste is made of hydrogen peroxide, dish soap, yeast and purple food coloring. It wouldn't taste very good."

"Yuck." agreed the class.

"How does that," Mitry pointed at the ingredients "make that?" She pointed at the Elephant Toothpaste.

"Elephant toothpaste is the result of a chemical reaction." replied Ms. Detore. "A chemical reaction is what happens when you mix different substances together and they turn into something new. In this experiment the water and oxygen in hydrogen peroxide reacts with the dish soap and the enzyme, catalyze, in yeast to create foam. The food coloring is what makes the foam purple."

Mitry looked down at the periodic table on her tablet. Oxygen (O) was number 8. Hydrogen (H) number 1. She didn't see catalase or enzyme anywhere.

"Ms. Detore, Ms. Detore!" Aiden, Mitry's best friend, waved his arms wildly. "Are chocolate chip cookies a chemical reaction? Because you have to mix a bunch of stuff to make cookies and then you have to bake them."

Aiden loved chocolate chip cookies. They were his favorite thing to eat and to talk about.

Ms. Detore laughed. "Yes, Aiden. Baking chocolate chip cookies involves chemical reactions, so does digesting them!"

Aiden's tummy growled at the thought of eating chocolate chip cookies.

"Chemical reactions between elements are happening all of the time, every day." Continued Ms. Detore, this time speaking to the whole class. "We came to the Science Museum today so that you can learn about the elements and chemical reactions that make substances like Elephant Toothpaste possible. Now that our demonstration is done, it's time to buddy up and explore!"

All of the kids, except Mitry and Aiden, scattered to look for buddies.

Aiden bumped Mitry with his shoulder.

"Buddy?" he asked.

"Buddy." she confirmed.

They did their best friend handshake.

The two closest exhibits; Metalloids and Halogens, were crowded with students. The two friends kept walking until they came to a wall with the words Noble Gases written across the top. None of their classmates had gone this far into the exhibit.

"Noble, that's like royalty right?" Asked Aiden.

Mitry scrunched her shoulders. "I dunno. Maybe. What does it say?"

Aiden continued reading off the wall.

When the Noble Gases were first discovered, scientists thought that they were rare and inert. This is why these elements were named the Rare Gases, Inert Gases and eventually the Noble Gases.

"Tablet," Aiden addressed his device. "What does inert mean?"

"Inert describes an element that has little or no ability to react with other elements." Answered the tablet.

There were six elements listed down the wall. Helium (He), Neon (Ne), Argon (Ar), Krypton (Kr), Xenon (Xe), and Radon (Rn). Mitry used her finger to circle the Noble Gases on her tablet.

"I'll take notes on Krypton, Xenon, and Radon if you take notes on Helium, Neon, and Argon." said Aiden.

Mitry looked at the wall of text and pictures and groaned. She hated taking notes.

"Ok." she mumbled.

Aiden squatted to get a better look at the paragraph on Radon. Mitry slumped her forehead against her tablet and slowly dragged it down her face.

When her eyes peeked out from behind her tablet she noticed a woman in a white lab coat further in the exhibit.

A scientist! A real-life scientist!

An interview with a scientist would be so much better than taking notes.

Mitry snuck a glance at Ms. Detore and her other classmates. They were still clustered around the

Halogens and Metalloids. Ms. Detore had said they weren't supposed to leave this section of the museum. If she left to follow the scientist she might get in trouble.

Mitry looked back over at the scientist. She was walking further and further away!

"I'll be quick!" thought Mitry to herself. *"Ms. Detore will never know!"*

"I'll be right back Aiden." said Mitry. She gave him their secret signal so he would know to cover for her. Then she turned and walked deeper into the exhibit.

CHAPTER 2

THE LAB

Wow! The museum was huge and the scientist was fast. Mitry followed her out of the Chemistry Exhibit, past a rocket ship in the Air & Space Exhibit and down a hallway in Biology before she finally caught up.

"Dr. Scientist!" she shouted. "Can I interview you?"

The scientist whirled around. The hair around her face was streaked with blue and purple. Those were Mitry's two favorite colors.

"Dr. Scientist." The scientist mused. "I like it! What is your name?"

Mitry told her.

"It is nice to meet you Mitry. I am Dr. Hathale. I'll give you an interview but I need to put this tray away first."

She lowered the lab tray she was holding so Mitry could see it better. In the middle of the tray there was a full test tube rack and an evaporation dish.

"Would you mind holding this tray while I open the door?"

Mitry's brown eyes lit up.

"Not at all!"

She tucked her tablet under her arm and held the tray while Dr. Hathale opened a door with a Staff Only sign. Mitry followed her inside.

Inside was a lab.

It was a large lab with multiple rows of white desks and shelves of lab supplies. The far wall had tall, wide windows that allowed museum visitors to look in. A balding scientist was peering into a microscope by the farthest window.

Dr. Hathale took the tray from Mitry and set it on one of the desks next to a folded lab coat and a pair of purple safety goggles.

"Okay, now that we've put the tray away I can interview you right?" Mitry asked

"That's right!" replied Dr. Hathale. "What's your first question?"

Mitry froze. She had been so excited about talking to a scientist that she hadn't put any thought into what to ask!

"Uhm."

Dr. Hathale waited patiently.

"Do you have any pets?" asked Mitry finally.

"Pets? I get to interview a scientist and my first question is about pets? I've blown it!" she thought.

Dr. Hathale giggled. "I do! How'd you guess? I have a labrador retriever named Rocket."

She pulled a picture of the brown puppy out from her lab coat. Mitry smiled, she hadn't blown it after all!

Dr. Hathale slipped Rocket's photo back into her pocket.

"Before we get to the rest of your questions, I should let your parents know where you are. Is there a number I can call?"

Mitry shook her head no.

"I came here with my teacher, Ms. Detore. She is in the Chemistry exhibit."

"I'll call her then. Wait here." Dr. Hathale spun on her heel and walked around the corner.

Mitry placed her tablet on the desk and sat down to wait. Her legs kicked back and forth and her fingers drummed on the chair. It was hard to sit still when she was this excited.

She could not believe she was in a real-life laboratory! Wait until she told Aiden! He'd want to come visit the laboratory too.

Mitry side-eyed the lab coat beside her on the desk.

Dr. Hathale probably wouldn't mind if she put it on, just for a little bit.

She grabbed the lab coat, stood up and put it on. It was too big but that didn't matter to Mitry. Even with the sleeves rolled up to her forearms like pool floaties she felt like a scientist. She grabbed the safety goggles and put them on to complete the look.

"Students," she said, imitating her teacher. "I am a scientist and I have spent my whole entire life studying..." she paused. What sort of scientist was she? She looked around the lab for inspiration.

On the wall opposite her there was a poster of the Periodic Table, just like on her tablet! She picked up her tablet and walked over to the poster.

"The Noble Gases." she addressed her imaginary audience. "I've spent my whole entire life studying the Noble Gases and I know everything about them."

The Noble Gases were on the far right hand side of the poster. She touched her hand against the colorful squares, letters and numbers.

The wall shuddered.

Mitry jumped back and looked around.

Did anybody else see that?

Suddenly, Mitry's ears filled with a buzzing sound.

Buzz, buzz, buzz.

A green light encircled her.

The air grew warm.

Then the lab began to spin.

"Dr. Hathale!" cried Mitry.

Her tablet slipped out from her sweaty hands and became a blur as it spun around her.

"Dr. Hathale! What's happening?"

There was no answer.

Mitry hugged her arms to her chest and squeezed her eyes shut. Her curls blew around wildly. She twisted around and around and around. Faster and faster.

The buzzing grew louder and louder.

The air grew warmer and warmer, and then, everything was still and quiet.

CHAPTER 3

TELEPORTATION TOWER

"She looks small for a scientist, doesn't she?"

"She is small, but she has a lab coat on so she must be a scientist."

Mitry opened her eyes.

In front of her were two metal, human-like figures. One was made of cylinders and curves and the other was made of cubes and angles. They were both staring at her questioningly.

"Robots!" She exclaimed.

"That's right!" They replied in unison.

"I'm Alternating Current, but you can call me AC." said the round one. It pointed to the cursive initials on its chest.

"And I'm Direct Current, but you can call me DC." said the angular one. It pointed to the block lettering on its chest.

Mitry introduced herself.

DC leaned forward.

"You are a scientist, aren't you Mitry?"

"We've been looking all across the universe for a scientist." added AC.

"And if you are not a scientist we will have to send you back."

Send her back?

Mitry looked around. She wasn't in Dr. Hathale's lab anymore. There were no desks or shelves of lab supplies. No museum visitors peering in or balding scientists quietly at work.

The walls of this room were green. The same shade of green that Mitry had seen right before Dr. Hathale's lab began to spin.

There was a large window and balcony to her right. Out the window, Mitry could see rolling hills and distant towns and cities.

To her left there was a giant three-paneled screen. A digital map was displayed across the three screens as if it was one screen. The map was zoomed in on the roof of the science museum. Mitry could see her school bus in the parking lot.

Above her was a machine that she had never seen before. It looked like a giant ceiling fan, but the center of it was glowing and the tips of the fan blades were bent toward her.

She looked down. She was laying in the middle of a red target.

AC and DC looked at her expectantly. They were waiting for an answer.

Mitry thought a moment.

"I am a scientist." she announced.

She stood up and adjusted her lab coat and safety goggles.

"Scientists come in all sizes and shapes."

"So do robots!" cried AC.

Mitry smiled in response. AC and DC were the first robots she had ever met and she liked them already.

They liked her too.

"We're so happy you're here!" DC assured her.

"Where exactly am I?" She asked. "This isn't the museum lab."

"This is Teleportation Tower." answered DC.

"And Teleportation Tower is in STEM-land. STEM-land is the most technologically advanced land in the universe." added DC.

"Well, at least we think so." clarified AC. "We haven't been to every land in the universe so we can't know for sure."

"I don't think. I KNOW." insisted DC.

DC looked up at Mitry eagerly. "Our brilliant leader, the Magician, knows everything there is to know about science, technology, engineering and math. No one is smarter than the Magician, that's how I know STEM-Land is the most technologically advanced land in the universe. The Magician told me it is!"

AC spiraled up into the air and patted one of the machine's blades.

"It *was* the Magician who built this teleporter." The robot admitted. "We wouldn't have been able to bring you here without it or without this remote." AC pulled a remote out from behind its back.

The remote only had two buttons. One green and one blue.

"One tap on the blue button while you're on that target and you'd go back home."

"But we wouldn't want that!" cried DC.

"You just got here! Don't you want to meet the Magician?"

Mitry had never met a magician before.

What a day this was turning out to be. She'd met a scientist, she'd visited a real lab, she'd befriended two robots and now she was going to meet a magician! Not just any magician, the smartest magician in the world, the inventor of a teleportation machine!

Ms. Detore might give her extra-credit for an interview with a magician.

"Let's go meet the Magician." she said.

AC and DC high-fived.

"Follow us!"

Mitry, AC and DC left the room.

Minutes later, Mitry's tablet tumbled down from the ceiling and crash landed on the red target in the middle of the floor.

CHAPTER 4

THE MAGICIAN

Halfway down the stairs Mitry stopped.

"Did you hear that?"

The two robots stopped humming rock music to themselves and looked at Mitry.

"Hear what?" asked AC.

"I didn't hear anything." replied DC.

"I thought I heard something fall, it sounded like something broke." Mitry looked back up the stairs. "Should we go back?"

Before AC and DC could respond there was a loud BEEP BEEP!

"Our ride!" exclaimed the robots. They raced down the stairs and Mitry raced after them.

A small car was waiting for the trio at the bottom of the stairs. It was a cheery yellow color and had a soft, rounded design like AC. The headlights and grill on the front of the car made it look like the car was smiling.

Mitry, AC, and DC climbed inside and put on their seatbelts.

Suddenly the car lurched forward.

Neither Mitry, AC, or DC had touched anything but the seatbelts.

"Who is driving?" Cried Mitry.

AC and DC looked at each other.

"The car."

"The car?"

"It drives itself." Chimed AC.

"The Magician made it that way." Explained DC.

"With some help." clarified AC.

"That's true." admitted DC. "Scientists like you, programmers, engineers, and mathematicians come to visit and work with the Magician all of the time."

"Leonardo Da Vinci, Ada Lovelace, Marie Daly," AC listed some names. "they've all been here."

Leonardo Da Vinci! Mitry knew that name from class. He was a famous Italian inventor, scientist, artist, and engineer from the Renaissance time period.

AC pointed out the window. "When they visit they all stay at the Glass Castle with the Magician."

Mitry looked where AC pointed.

The castle was made of glass towers of varying heights. From far away the towers looked like a cluster of flasks, tubes, and beakers.

Next to the towers floated brightly colored dots.

Mitry squinted to try and see them more clearly.

"Are those balloons?" she asked.

"Hot gas balloons." The robots answered together.

"They're filled with a gas called Helium. Since Helium is less dense than air, the balloons float."

Helium! That was one of the Noble Gases that Mitry was supposed to take notes on. She looked around for her tablet. When she couldn't find it she scrunched her face and thought really hard about what she'd just learned so that she would remember it later.

There was a lot to remember! The city surrounding the Glass Castle was unlike any Mitry had ever visited before.

In addition to their self-driving car, there were self-driving trains and planes and hover-cars. People in strange clothes weaved through the streets on electric unicycles. Other people ate picnics under giant mechanical sunflowers that tracked the sun and generated power from solar panel petals.

Mitry had no problem coming up with questions this time! Yet no matter what she asked, whether it was how something worked or how something was made the robots had the same answer. It was the Magician. The Magician was behind every wonder in not just this city but all of STEM-land.

The car came to a stop at the foot of the Glass Castle.

"We're here!" exclaimed AC and DC.

Together they left the car in a tidy, garden court-yard and walked inside.

The castle was packed with people, some in chairs and some standing. Their attention was focused on a stage at the far end of the room.

On the stage stood a blonde woman. She was dressed in a sparkly red tuxedo and matching top hat. In her silk gloved hand she held a wand.

"Welcome! One and all to today's magical showcase! Is everyone ready to see some magic?" She shouted.

"Huzzah!" Shouted the crowd, AC, and DC.

"Huzzah!" echoed Mitry.

"For today's trick, I will need an assistant." announced the Magician.

She looked over the crowd of raised hands.

Cries of "Pick me!" Pick me!" echoed around the room.

"You." She pointed her wand at Mitry.

A spotlight angled down at the 3rd grader.

"Me?" Asked Mitry.

"Yes, you. What is your name?"

"Mitry." She replied.

"Well, Mitry, would you please come up to the stage?"

Everyone started clapping.

"What an honor!" gushed AC and DC as they walked Mitry up the stairs to the stage.

Mitry scrunched her eyes. The lighting made it hard to see the crowd.

On the stage, the magician pointed her wand at two large glass tanks of liquid. One tank was labeled Tank A and the other was labeled Tank B. The top half of the tanks had clear liquid and the bottom half of the tanks had dark blue liquid. A divider within the tanks kept the two liquids from mixing.

21

Beside each tank hung a braided gold rope.

"Mitry, please pull on the rope next to Tank A. Pull it as hard as you can." Instructed the Magician.

Mitry grabbed the rope with both hands and gave it a good yank.

With a loud whoosh the divider in Tank A opened up.

Instantly the clear and dark blue liquids mixed together turning the entire tank light blue.

"Once the divider is removed only a powerful magician can prevent the clear liquid from mixing with the blue liquid." The Magician told the crowd.

She tipped her hat toward the front row and winked.

"Luckily, I am the most powerful magician of all."

The crowd cheered. They agreed!

"For this magical feat I will prevent the liquids from mixing with three taps from my wand."

The Magician climbed up a ladder and tapped her wand over the top of Tank B once, twice, three times.

"Mitry, pull the rope!" She shouted.

Like before, Mitry pulled the rope next to the tank.

There was a big whoosh and the divider in Tank B opened up.

The liquids did not mix! Tank B was clear on top and blue on bottom as if the divider was still there.

Mitry gasped.

The crowd oohed and ahhed.

AC and DC clapped wildly.

The Magician bowed.

Then a dark curtain fell blocking Mitry, AC, DC, and the Magician from the crowd's view.

CHAPTER 5

THE NOBLE GASES

CRACK! BOOM! WHIZZ! POP!

Colorful spirals burst from the broken tablet. They spun, twisted and exploded around the room in all directions like fireworks.

From the spirals came a parade of characters. A copper spiral dissolved into a band of heavy metal rockers playing air guitars. A gold spiral turned into a miner with a beard and a pickaxe.

"We're free!" Exclaimed a pilot as she flew by in a silvery twin-engine plane.

Free?

It was true. The elements from the periodic table weren't just pictures on a chart anymore. They were 3D and as much a part of the world as the tablet they'd been released from.

Helium adjusted his glasses and looked around. Most of the elements were bouncing off the walls, out the broken window or down the stairs. He twitched his walrus mustache disapprovingly. All of this commotion seemed like an overreaction to him.

In the middle of the chaos were five gaseous elements that, like Helium, didn't have much of a reaction to being free.

It was the rest of his family, the Noble Gases; Neon (NE), Krypton (KR), Xenon (XE), Radon (RN), and Argon (AR). With the exception of Krypton, their abbreviations were proudly worn on sashes across their chests.

Normally colorless each of the Noble Gases had taken on a color of their own in STEM-Land. Neon was a flashy pink, Krypton was green, Xenon was purple, Radon was radioactive yellow, and Argon was blue.

The Noble Gases were not known for mixing with other elements. They were quite happy all on their own, but in the rare instances they had to socialize they preferred each other's company. After all, they were family and had qualities in common.

This chaotic situation was one of those rare circumstances where the Noble Gases did not want to be on their own.

Helium floated over to the other Noble Gases adding his redness to their colorful display.

"Ladies, gentlemen" He tucked an arm behind his back and bowed.

"Lord Helium," the other Noble Gases acknowledged his arrival with bows and curtsies.

"I trust that you have agreed on a noble quest?" Helium inquired in his high, squeaky voice. Family meetings were often focused around noble deeds like quests.

"Perhaps," replied Xenon in her deep, low voice. From a hidden pocket in her petticoat she pulled out the two broken halves of the tablet.

"This is the fabled Tablet of Knowledge. Before it broke in half it could summon for its user all of the information in the world."

Helium, although amazed, did not visibly express his amazement. As a noble, he was above such reactions.

Xenon flipped one of the halves over. On the back there was a white label with the name Mitry in black lettering.

Argon spoke up. "Our noble quest is to return the Tablet of Knowledge to its rightful owner so that its powers can be used to benefit the universe." He tapped on the name with his cane. "We must find Mitry."

"Hear, hear!" cried the Noble Gases in agreement.

Radon started coughing loudly. He wasn't much of a talker but when he did talk it always started with a coughing fit.

"How will we do it? How will we find Mitry?" he coughed out the words. His many medals and ribbons of valor jumped up and down against his chest with every cough.

The other Noble Gases fell silent. Radon had asked

good questions. *How* would they find Mitry? They didn't even know what Mitry looked like!

Krypton put down her comic book to think. She wondered what her favorite superheroes would do in this situation.

Neon looked around the room. Maybe she'd see something, a sign that would point her in the right direction.

Helium tried to think but his thoughts were in outer space. He couldn't come up with anything!

Radon stroked his sideburns in quiet thought.

"I've got it!" Argon exclaimed. He lifted up his top hat to reveal a bright, shining lightbulb.

"The castle," he pointed out the window at a glass castle in the distance "where there are castles there are nobles."

"And nobles know about everything and everyone who passes through their lands." exclaimed Krypton She'd caught on to Argon's idea.

"Exactly!" cried Argon.

The nobles in the Glass Castle would help them find Mitry and complete their quest.

"To the Glass Castle!" cried Helium.

"Hear, hear!" answered the Noble Gases.

Helium, Xenon, Krypton, Neon, and Radon floated over to the broken window. One by one they passed through a hole into the open air until only Argon was left inside.

Argon poked his head out the window.

"I admit the Glass Castle is a lot farther away than I realized."

A breeze ruffled the tails of his coat. He shivered.

"And it's so cold outside. That is no good, no good at all. I don't conduct heat very well, you know that."

The Noble Gases smiled at one another. They had known Argon for a long time and they knew that he was lazy. On the periodic table he was known as Argon the Inactive.

The lightbulb above his head started flashing again.

"I've got an idea!" he said, "I'll stay here, just in case Mitry comes back!"

Now, that was a bright idea!

CHAPTER 6

BEHIND THE
CURTAIN

Mitry, AC, DC, and the Magician basked in the thunderous applause. The crowd had loved the show!

When the applause finally ended, AC and DC scooped up the flowers that had been thrown on the stage and placed them in a large wicker basket.

"That was my best show this month!" Shared the Magician. "I saw jaws drop! I think some people fell out of their chairs!"

She turned to face Mitry. "Thank you for your help. You were a wonderful assistant."

Mitry beamed. Not only was she a scientist, now she was also an experienced magician's assistant.

"How did you do it?" she asked. "Is your wand really magic?"

The Magician's bright red lips spread out into a smile.

"You're so curious! I should have guessed that you'd ask about my magic trick. Scientists always do." She winked at AC and DC over Mitry's shoulder.

"I don't normally reveal my tricks to non-magicians." she continued looking down at Mitry, "but since you are a scientist I will make an exception. After all, a scientist is just a magician without showmanship."

The Magician took Mitry's hand, turned her palm over and tapped it three times with her wand. One, two, three!

Nothing happened.

The wand was nothing more than painted wood!

"Surprised?" asked the Magician.

"Yes, and confused." admitted Mitry. "I thought the wand was magic."

"The magic isn't in the wand." The Magician pointed the tip of the wand at her temple. "The magic is in here," She pointed the wand at Mitry's forehead. "And in here. You see, the magic is in what you know and in what others don't."

The Magician twirled around to address the robots.

"AC, DC please read off my magician notes on the back of the Tanks."

AC standing behind Tank A read aloud. "Tank A contains equal amounts of blue-dyed water in the bottom compartment and non-dyed water in the top compartment."

DC poked his head out from behind Tank B. "Tank B contains equal amounts of blue-dyed water in the bottom compartment and non-dyed vegetable oil in the top compartment."

Vegetable oil!

"Vegetable oil is less dense than water." explained the Magician. "When you combine the same amount of liquids with different densities the liquid with the lower density will always float on top of the liquid with greater density."

Density! That was the same reason that the hot gas balloons Mitry had seen earlier could float. The helium in the balloons made them less dense than the air around them.

"Wait a second, that's not magic, that's just science!"

The Magician laughed. It was an infectious, loud laugh that filled the whole stage.

"Just science? Mitry! Science isn't *just* anything. Science *is* the thing! Science is the reason I knew that trick would work. Science is how I know that trick will work *every* time I perform it."

The Magician continued. "I have other magic tricks. Tricks where I bend water, tie it in knots and make it disappear. Tricks where I turn white flowers into purple flowers, blue flowers. Mitry, I can turn flowers into any color you want! All of these tricks are possible because of science."

The Magician took both of Mitry's hands and squeezed them tight.

"Everything that we think is magic is science that we haven't learned yet. The more science we learn the more magic we can create."

Mitry thought about the Elephant Toothpaste, the hot gas balloons and the Magician's density magic trick. She had learned so much science already. Perhaps she could become a magician one day too.

As the Magician talked she used her grip on Mitry's hands to guide her toward the center of the stage.

"I'm so happy that you are here Mitry. You see, I have another showcase coming up and I'm afraid I'll look like a fool if I don't have any new magic to show off. I really don't want to look like a fool. I want everyone to keep thinking that I am the smartest in all of STEM-Land."

She looked pleadingly at Mitry. "All of the other scientists, engineers, mathematicians, and programmers have stopped visiting. They didn't understand why I wouldn't let them teach anyone else the magic tricks, but that doesn't matter now because I have you Mitry! With your help, your science knowledge and my showmanship there's no telling what magic we can create!"

"*My* help?" asked Mitry in surprise. Being a magician's assistant was one thing, but helping her create magic tricks? Could Mitry really do that?

"Oh yes, you're the only one who can help me." The Magician assured her.

The Magician made everything seem so grand and exciting. Mitry was happy she had found herself on this adventure and that she could help the Magician when others had refused to help. The Magician made Mitry feel special. She could barely wait to tell her family, Ms. Detore, Dr. Hathale, and Aiden about everything she had seen, been, and done.

Thinking of her family and friends reminded her how long she'd been gone. She had told Aiden that she'd be right back! She hoped he wasn't mad about waiting so long for her to return.

"I'd be happy to help." she told the Magician. "I'll study tonight at home and then we can create new magic tricks tomorrow."

"Home?" questioned the Magician. "Why would you go home when I have everything a scientist could possibly need right here in the Glass Castle? No, you won't go home. You're going to stay here as my honored guest."

Mitry tried to back away but the Magician would not let go of her hands.

"Let me go!" cried Mitry. "I don't want to stay here. Let me go!"

She yelled for her new robot friends AC and DC.

"AC, DC, help me!"

The two robots looked at each other uncomfortably but stayed where they were on the stage.

"Let me go!" Mitry yelled again as she tried to twist and turn out of the Magician's grasp.

"As you wish," replied the Magician. Then she whispered a magic word and released Mitry's hands.

With a gasp, the 3rd grader disappeared beneath the stage.

CHAPTER 7

THE MAKERSPACE

WHUMP!
　　Mitry landed in a giant bean bag.
　　She glared at the ceiling.

Above her was a sealed trapdoor. The Magician, AC, and DC had planned this all along!

"This isn't going to work you know!" she shouted "You can trap me, but you can't make me help you!"

There was no answer.

Mitry climbed out of the bean bag to examine her surroundings.

This room was ablaze with color. The walls, floor, and parts of the ceiling had been painted with bright zig-zags, checkermarks, squiggles, stripes, polka-dots and shiny spirals. Someone had even painted a hopscotch on the floor!

Plastic cubbies lined one of the walls. There were cubbies full of popsicle sticks, rubber bands, magnets, cardboard, yarn, tape, scissors, screwdrivers, beads and much more. Next to the cubbies sat a tower of wooden blocks.

On one of the walls, someone had mounted a giant plastic swordfish. A red ball was stuck to his bill which made the swordfish look clownish. On another wall there was a broken, old-fashioned clock. The long hand was missing and the short hand wasn't moving.

In the center of the room was the bean bag she had landed in and a workbench with an embedded screen.

Other than the trap door there didn't appear to be any way in or out. There were no windows or doors. There was a vent on the ground in the final hopscotch square but it was too small for Mitry to fit through.

What sort of lab was this? Where were the microscopes? What good were rubber bands and popsicle sticks? This room didn't look anything like Dr. Hathale's lab or Teleportation Tower.

She walked over to the workbench and tapped on the screen. Maybe she could connect to the internet and message someone back home!

"*Welcome to the Glass Castle Makerspace.*" The words unfurled across the screen.

So, that's what this place was; a makerspace. Mitry tapped back to the homescreen.

The words *Density Magic Trick* were already in the search bar. She tapped search and a long list of different density experiments and magic tricks appeared on the page. A green check mark icon appeared next to each one. A record had been kept so that no magic tricks would be repeated. The Magician was only interested in new magic tricks.

"Trap door magic trick." she commanded the screen.

The trap door was the only way in or out that she could see so that's what she was going to focus on.

"Searching." responded the screen assistant as it combed through all of the experiments.

It brought up only one result; FAILED EXPERI-MENTS was written across it in bright red.

"Open up a trap door" she tried again.

FAILED EXPERIMENTS.

"Reverse engineer a trap door!" she shouted.

FAILED EXPERIMENTS. The bright red font screamed back at her.

Her face twisted up and grew hot. Her breathing became huffy. She looked up at the ceiling to avoid crying.

If all of the other scientists, engineers, mathematicians, and programmers had failed at opening the trap door, what chance did she have? She wasn't a real scientist. She'd only been pretending. She wasn't actually smart. She was just a dumb kid!

Tears spilled out of her eyes and tumbled down her cheeks. She missed her parents, Aiden, Ms. Detore and Dr. Hathale. She wanted to go home!

If only she could snap her fingers and transport herself home, like magic!

Magic.

The Magician's speech played in Mitry's mind.

Magic is only science we haven't learned yet.

The Magician had learned all of her magic tricks

from scientists, engineers, mathematicians, and programmers. She had learned from their successes, perhaps Mitry could learn from their failures.

She closed her eyes and clicked on the bright red FAILED EXPERIMENTS link.

"You're done it!" boomed a voice from the screen.

Mitry blinked. That wasn't the screen assistant's voice!

She looked down at the screen.

The FAILED EXPERIMENTS link had opened up a secret video.

The video was zoomed in on an older man. He had a bushy grey-streaked beard, a grease-smeared forehead and smile wrinkles in the corners of his eyes.

He was smiling up from the screen at Mitry.

"You took a brave step by clicking on that FAILED EXPERIMENTS link. Failure is a scary thing! It bruises the ego because it means we aren't as smart or as strong or as clever as we thought we were."

Mitry sure hadn't felt smart when that bright red FAILED EXPERIMENTS link had popped up not once but three times!

"Failure means we have much to learn. If you're brave enough to press on after failure then you may be brave enough to learn something new, something that will help you turn your failure into a success story."

Mitry looked around the room. There still weren't any windows or doors. The vent on the ground was still too small for her to fit through and the trap door was still sealed shut. Her impossible situation hadn't changed, but she was starting to change. She was feeling brave and hopeful. She was going to figure this out. She was ready to learn!

The old man tapped on the fabric name tag that had been stitched to his denim shirt. It said Mike in red lettering.

"The name is Mike. I'm a maker. I'm part of a crew of makers. We were trapped in the Glass Castle Makerspace once too, but we made our escape out the Disappearing Door."

A disappearing door!

"To find the Disappearing Door you'll need to build a black-light device, to get started solve for the secret code my crew and I left for you in the cubbies. You'll want to hurry because time is short. The Magician will expect a new magic trick from you soon."

Mitry repeated the instructions to herself.

Mike raised his hand to his forehead in a salute.

"Good luck fellow maker. I hope to see you outside these walls soon."

The video shut off.

"Excuse me, my lady. Are you a Noble?"

Mitry's head jolted up.

Floating in the air above her were five gases dressed like lords and ladies from Victorian England.

"What are you? Who are you? Where did you come from?" Mitry blurted out all of her questions at once.

"We are the Noble Gases." replied the one directly

across from Mitry. He had a high-pitched, cartoony voice. Mitry let out a giggle before slapping a hand over her mouth.

"My name is Helium" continued the red gas with the funny voice, "and this is Krypton, Xenon, Neon, and Radon."

"We got here through the vent." added Neon helpfully. Bright neon pink arrows appeared all around the vent, they flashed for a few moments and then disappeared.

The Noble Gases? Those were the elements she and Aiden were supposed to take notes on. How was any of this possible?

Mitry crossed her arms defensively. She wasn't sure if she trusted these "so-called" Noble Gases. "If you're here to check on me you can tell the Magician I meant what I said. I'm not going to help her."

Krypton poked her head up from the comic book she was always reading. "Magician?" She asked. "Sounds like a villain." She tapped her comic, "I would know. I'm an expert on battles between good and evil, bad guys and good guys."

Xenon looked at Mitry with big, comforting eyes from beneath her floppy hat. "We don't know of any Magician." She assured her with a gentle pat on the arm. "We're looking for Mitry."

How did they know her name? Mitry was more suspicious now.

"Why are you looking for Mitry?" she asked.

Xenon pulled out the broken tablet from her petticoat.

"We're trying to return this to her. It's broken, but we thought she might be able to fix it."

"That's mine!" exclaimed Mitry. She grabbed the two halves of her school tablet from Xenon.

"I don't think I'll be able to fix it." she remarked looking at the damage. "Where did you find it?"

"Teleportation Tower." answered Neon. The other Noble Gases looked at her. "I saw a sign." she explained.

"Teleportation Tower!" Mitry cried. "I'm trying to get back there! It's my only way home."

"Then allow us to rescue you." said Helium gallantly. As a Noble Gas he was fond of noble deeds and now that they had found Mitry they were in need of another noble deed. There were few deeds more noble than a rescue. "If you'd just follow us back through the vent we can take you there."

"I won't fit." said Mitry. "I'm not a gas like all of you."

"She makes a solid point." quipped Krypton.

Deflated, the Noble Gases sunk down to sit around the table with Mitry.

"It's okay." Mitry assured her new friends.

"I know how we can get out of here, together."

CHAPTER 8

THE DISAPPEARING DOOR

Mike the Maker had told them that the secret code was in the cubbies so Mitry and the Noble Gases started there.

After some rummaging Radon, wheezing, held up a golden envelope he'd found in a cubbie full of coffee beans.

Mitry opened the golden envelope and spread the code out on the table.

"Oh no!" she exclaimed.

"It's a computer code!"

```
var blockSymbol = 'balloon';
if (blockSymbol === 'balloon') {
print ('Jump three times on hopscotch square 1');
}
if (blockSymbol !== 'balloon') {
```

```
print ('Tickle the swordfish's belly');
}
```

The Noble Gases peered over Mitry's shoulder and confirmed that she was right. They were looking at a coding language called javascript.

"It's not fair. I don't know how to read this. Why can't the code be something I already know?"

Frustrated Mitry pushed the paper away from her.

Every time she thought she'd figured something out a new problem popped up. It was exhausting and it made her feel stupid.

She remembered what Mike the Maker had said about learning from failure. How many times would she have to fail before she knew enough to get out of the Makerspace? 5 times? 10? 100?

Gently, Xenon slid the paper back toward Mitry.

"You're always going to have to learn," she said, "but you don't have to figure everything out by yourself. We can help."

"Let's start with the first line." suggested Neon helpfully.

var blockSymbol = 'balloon' lit up in neon pink.

Mitry read the line out loud. None of them knew what var meant but they all knew what a balloon was. That left blockSymbol for them to figure out. What was blockSymbol and how did it equal balloon? How could anything equal a balloon that wasn't a balloon? Equal meant the same as, didn't it?

"blockSymbol, blockSymbol, blockSymbol...Oh!"

All heads turned to Krypton. She was hovering next to the tower of wooden blocks near the cubbies. One of the blocks was in her hand. A sun symbol was painted on the side of it.

"It's a block, with a symbol on it." she explained. "I think we need to find the block with a balloon symbol."

Of course! Mitry and the Noble Gases started counting up the blocks and checking all of the symbols. There were blocks with stars, rain clouds, flowers, and other symbols but none of the blocks had a balloon.

Mitry and the Noble Gases returned to the computer code. There was more that they needed to figure out.

```
var blockSymbol = 'balloon';
if (blockSymbol === 'balloon') {
print ('Jump three times on hopscotch square 1');
}
if (blockSymbol !== 'balloon') {
print ('Tickle the swordfish's belly');
}
```

"Well, the first line means block with a balloon. I don't think we got that wrong." Mitry and the Noble Gases agreed on that.

"Let's try line number 2." suggested Xenon.

"If," read Mitry, "block with a balloon print jump three times on hopscotch square 1."

"There aren't any blocks with balloons." said Helium. He had been the most disappointed about that. He loved balloons.

Mitry read the next lines, "If block with balloon print tickle the swordfish belly."

What sort of code was this? It told her two different things to do if she had a block with a balloon but nothing to do if she didn't have a block with a balloon.

"Wait a second. I don't think that's right."

Neon pointed at the computer code and two neon pink boxes appeared. One box around the === in the first set of instructions and one box around the !=== in the second set of instructions.

"See, these are different. What if the last set of lines actually means block without balloon not block with balloon?"

Mitry looked at the code. The exclamation in front of the equal signs had made her pause when she first read the code aloud. Maybe it did mean block without balloon. If that's what it meant then the instructions she had to follow was to tickle the swordfish's belly.

"Xenon! Tickle that swordfish!" Mitry pointed a finger at the plastic fish on the wall.

Xenon dusted the swordfish with her lace hanky and then tickled the belly. There was a click then a flap swung open from the underside of the fish. Xenon reached inside and pulled out another gold envelope and a smartwatch.

They'd done it! They'd solved the first clue!

Mitry slipped the smartwatch on to her wrist then

tapped the tiny screen. It lit up revealing an assortment of apps against a blue background. Now they didn't have to fix the tablet or drag the workbench computer along with them.

Next, Mitry picked up the golden envelope and ripped it open revealing two math problems.

Problem #1	Problem #2
12	928
x 3	- 103

"Two-digit multiplication and three-digit subtraction. She looked up at the Noble Gases.

"I've only done single-digit multiplication and subtraction." She admitted, "Single-digit problems were hard for me at first but Ms. Detore helped me figure out how to solve them, just like all of you helped me solve the computer code."

She thought a moment.

"We may fail the first time, maybe even the second, but we will solve these problems." She said confidently.

"Hear! Hear!" cried the Noble Gases in support.

Mitry grabbed a handful of beads from a cubbie.

"If I was solving a single digit multiplication problem, like 3 x 2, I could make 3 piles of 2 beads each or I could make 2 piles of 3 beads each." She spread the beads out on the workbench. "They'd both use 6 beads because 3 x 2 and 2 x 3 both equal 6." She explained to the Noble Gases.

Krypton put her comic book away and pushed her

glasses back up her nose. She wanted to learn too!

"Basically, a multiplication problem tells me how many groups and how many beads per group and then asks how many beads there are total." Mitry divided the beads into 3 groups of 12 beads each and counted them up. There were 36 beads in total.

She wrote 36 under Problem #1 then turned her attention to Problem #2.

Xenon floated over her shoulder. "Problem #2 looks like it's going to take more beads than we have." She remarked.

Mitry agreed.

"Let's try breaking it up into smaller parts, like we broke up the computer code. 8-3=5." She wrote 5 under Problem #2.

Krypton carefully counted out 8 beads and then Neon took away 3 of them leaving Krypton with 5 beads. The math checked out!

Mitry quickly solved the rest of the problem.

Problem #1	Problem #2
12	928
x 3	- 103
36	825

Helium squeaked "36-825, we have a code!"

"Now we need to make a black-light."

"I've found one search result for black-light." Spoke the screen assistant from the workbench computer.

Mitry and the Noble Gases peered over the instructions. They needed a smartwatch, tape, a purple marker and a blue marker."

Krypton scooped up the tape and markers in her school-girl cap and floated them over to the workbench.

Following the instructions, Mitry placed a small strip of clear, sticky tape over the smartwatch's LED light. Neon took the blue marker and colored the piece of tape blue. When she was done, Mitry carefully placed another piece of tape on top of the first piece and Neon colored that piece blue too. Then Xenon added the third and final piece of tape and colored that piece purple.

Now they had a black-light device!

Helium flipped a light-switch they had found and plunged the Makerspace into darkness.

Mitry enabled the flashlight app. Slowly, she panned the black-light around the room.

"Do you see anything?" Krypton asked in a whisper.

"Nothing, nothing," murmured Xenon, "still nothing."

"THERE!" Exclaimed Neon. She lit up brilliantly bathing Mitry and the other Noble Gases in neon light.

"Too bright, too bright!" Xenon cried as she shielded her eyes with her floppy hat. Neon dimmed her lights so that it was dark enough again for Mitry and the other Noble Gases to see.

On the wall below the broken clock was the

painted outline of a door. When Mitry moved the black-light the outline disappeared. It was the Disappearing Door!

Mitry and the Noble Gases moved over to it. There was no handle or keypad.

"How do we open it? Where do we enter the code?" asked Radon between coughing fits.

Mitry recited Mike the Maker's clues to herself. Solve for the secret code in the cubbies? Check. Create a black-light? Check. Hurry, because time is short...

"Time is short!" cried Mitry.

"Well, it's relative actually." corrected Krypton.

Mitry tilted the black-light up so that it shown on the broken clock. "Look! The clock only has a short hand. I think the clock is actually a lock and the short hand is how we enter the code."

Helium wasn't convinced. "The clock only has numbers 1 through 12. The first two numbers of the code are greater than 12."

"What if we broke the code up into smaller numbers? Like we broke the computer code and the math problems into smaller pieces?" asked Krypton, "so the code is 3-6-8-2-5 instead of 36-825."

It was worth a shot!

Helium floated up to the clock. He spun the short hand around three times and then stopped it at the 3. Then he moved the short hand to the left all the way around past the 3 and he stopped it at the 6. Then he moved the short hand to the right and so on until he'd entered all 5 numbers.

Creeaakk!

The Disappearing Door swung open. They'd done it!

CHAPTER 9

A LASER LIGHT
BATTLE

Mitry and the Noble Gases rushed through the Disappearing Door and out into a long hallway. The hallway lights were bright and flashing. An alarm blared loudly.

"That alarm must be because of us." worried Xenon.

"Let's run!" cried Mitry.

The group of friends sped down the hall past portraits of the Magician and visiting engineers, mathematicians, programmers, and scientists. In all of the portraits the Magician and her guest had an invention on display and their arms were full of flowers and trophies.

The farther down the hall they went the grumpier the engineers, mathematicians, programmers, and scientists became and the more space the Magician took up in the portraits.

By the time they got to the end of the hall the Magician was the only one left in the portraits. Her arms full of flowers and trophies.

Mitry stopped in front of the last portrait. She looked to the left and she looked to the right. Which way to go?

Two familiar voices interrupted her thoughts.

"How did this happen?"

"I don't know! We certainly didn't bring those elements here."

"We only brought Mitry."

"Could she have brought the elements with her?"

"Whether she did or she didn't, they're here and they're our problem now!"

It was AC and DC and they were headed her way!

"To the left!" Mitry decided. She and the Noble Gases turned to the left just as AC and DC appeared around the corner on their right.

"Elements!" exclaimed AC.

"Mitry!" exclaimed DC.

"She's escaped!" exclaimed the robots in unison.

"RUN!" Mitry yelled as loud as she could.

The friends bolted; zigging and zagging and turning corners everywhere they could to try and lose the robots behind them.

"They're catching up!" Helium warned.

They were coming up to another split in the hallway. This time the hall split into three directions, straight, left, and right. If they could get a large enough lead on AC and DC they'd be able to disappear down one of those directions without being seen.

"Helium, Neon, Xenon, Krypton, Argon!" huffed Mitry. "We need a distraction. Something to slow them down and stop them from seeing where we go!"

Xenon glowed. "I believe I've had a flash of brilliance." she exclaimed.

She flipped around to face the robots while the other Noble Gases and Mitry sped on ahead.

"It's a shame you aren't noble robots." she said. "Your future could have been so bright!" At the word "bright" the air around Xenon burst with blinding flashes and strobe lights. AC and DC blinked and stumbled into the walls and then into each other. Those bright lights had made them dizzy!

"Xenon!" cried Mitry when Xenon caught up with the group. "How did you do that?"

Before Xenon could answer Mitry's smartwatch responded.

Xenon is used to produce an intense, bright light. Xenon can be found in strobe lights, photographer's flash lamps, deep-sea exploration lights, motion picture lights and many other lamps.

Mitry had so much to learn about her new friends!

"Where are we now?" wheezed Radon.

They were outside the castle in a tidy, garden courtyard.

"I've been here before!" It was the same courtyard where AC, DC, and Mitry had parked their self-driving car when they arrived at the castle, but now the car was nowhere to be seen.

Beyond the gate, faraway in the distance Mitry could see Teleportation Tower.

It was too far to run, especially after all of the running they'd done already. She yanked on the locked gate. Even if it were close enough to run they'd have to get through the gate first!

She looked back at the hall they had come from. It would not be long before the robots caught up with them.

Helium and the other Noble Gases surrounded Mitry.

"If only you were lighter than air like us." remarked Xenon. "Flying is a much faster way to travel, and then you could just float over the gate."

Mitry grinned. She had an idea. Before the Noble Gases could ask about her idea Mitry had darted back into the castle and into the showroom where the Magician had performed her magic tricks.

When she returned to the courtyard she had a large wicker basket of roses under one arm and a stage curtain under the other.

In front of the Noble Gases, she set the curtain down on the ground and dumped the roses out of the basket.

"We're going to fly there in a balloon!"

Helium's chest swelled up with happiness. He loved balloons.

Mitry and the Noble Gases piled into the basket she had found. Then they tied the curtain's edges to four-points along the basket.

"Ready?" asked Helium.

"Ready!" replied Mitry and the Noble Gases.

Helium blew into the curtain filling it with lightweight helium gas.

"Stop them!"

The Magician, AC, and DC had caught up.

"Stop them, stop them, stop them!" shouted the Magician. She stomped her shiny black boots harder with each order.

AC and DC ran towards the make-shift hot gas balloon. They were almost to the basket when the curtain balloon swooped Mitry and the Noble Gases high up into the air.

The Noble Gases cheered.

"Whew!" Mitry let out a big breath. "We got out just in time."

"I see Teleportation Tower." Neon pointed at the tall tower with her feather boa. Little neon arrows flickered toward Teleportation Tower and then faded away.

"I see it too." said Xenon. "It looks like we're headed in the right direction."

"Good." Mitry yawned. All of that running had tired her out and the rocking of the basket was making her sleepy.

Some time later Mitry woke with a jolt.

The basket was wildly swaying side to side. It tipped so far to one side she almost tumbled out!

"What's happening?" cried Mitry.

"We're under attack!"

Ashley McAlpin

The Magician, AC, and DC had caught up with Mitry and the Noble Gases. They were on-board a blimp and had tied their aircraft to the balloon basket with hooked ropes.

As Mitry watched, AC and DC started pulling on the ropes to bring the aircraft closer.

"Radon, Mitry throw those hooks back!" shouted Krypton. Radon and Mitry scrambled to grab the hooks. "Neon, Xenon and I will buy us some time!"

With that, Krypton tore off her glasses and ripped open her shirt revealing another shirt with a giant, green Kr.

Then Xenon, Neon, and Krypton leapt into heroic action releasing bright flashing lights and lasers.

From the blimp the Magician released lasers of her own. The sky lit up with white, purple, blue, and green lights.

Radon and Mitry were tossing hooks overboard left and right but they couldn't keep up with how many there were. The blimp was pulling itself closer and closer. Soon AC and DC would be able to jump from the blimp to the balloon.

"Looks like you could use some help!"

Mitry turned around. She didn't recognize that voice.

A silvery twin-engine plane zipped into the space between the blimp and the balloon. In the cockpit was a pilot and a german shepherd in a combat helmet.

"It's Aluminum and Tin!"

Aluminum and Tin are part of the post-transition metals on the periodic table, also known as the poor, or other metals. Chirped Mitry's watch.

Aluminum saluted the Noble Gases and then trained her plane on the Magician's blimp. Pow-pow-pow! Her tiny plane fired little bullets of aluminum and tin at the blimp. "Woof, woof!" barked Tin from the rear seat of the plane.

"I've had enough of these elements! I'm not going to let them foil my plans!" screamed the Magician. Her white-gloved hands were balled into angry fists. "AC, DC, board that balloon and take down that plane!"

Before they could do anything another element came to the rescue.

"Jump!" cried the unfamiliar voice.

"It's Argon!" exclaimed Neon.

At the sound of their fellow Noble Gas' name, Helium, Xenon, Radon, and Krypton turned around.

Their balloon was just a few feet above the tower. They could see Argon standing on the balcony. In his hand he held the remote to the teleportation machine.

"Jump!" He yelled again.

Mitry and the rest of the Noble Gases shared a look and then they leapt out of their make-shift hot gas balloon and onto the balcony.

Without Helium the balloon couldn't stay afloat. It dropped to the ground with a loud crash.

Mitry and the Noble Gases ran into Teleportation

Tower. Aluminum and Tin were holding the Magician, AC, and DC back but they wouldn't be able to hold them back forever. Mitry and the Noble Gases did not have time to waste!

Mitry took her place on the red target with the Noble Gases right beside her.

The friends locked hands and closed their eyes.

"Argon!" Mitry shouted. "Press the blue button!"

CHAPTER 10

MITRY SAYS GOODBYE

The walls shuddered.

Mitry's ears filled with a buzzing sound.

Buzz, buzz, buzz.

A blue light encircled the red target.

The air grew warm.

Then the room began to spin.

It spun faster and faster.

The buzzing grew louder and louder.

The air warmer and warmer, and then, everything was still and quiet.

Mitry opened her eyes.

She was in a large lab with multiple rows of white desks and shelves of lab supplies. The far wall had tall, wide windows that allowed museum visitors to look in. A balding scientist was peering into a microscope by the farthest window.

She was back in the museum lab.

Mitry looked to her left.

There, on the table was Dr. Hathale's tray just where she'd left it. The test tube rack, test tubes, and evaporation dish on the tray were untouched.

It was as if Mitry had never gone to STEM-Land.

"Yes!" She danced wiggling her arms in the air and tapping her feet.

"We made it back!"

She twirled around to hug the Noble Gases but they weren't there.

"Helium? Neon? Argon?" Her voice became shaky as she named each of her friends and they didn't respond. "Radon? Xenon? Krypton? Can you hear me?"

Dr. Hathale poked her head out from around the corner "I got in contact with your teacher, Ms. Detore, she's waiting for us in the Chemistry Exhibit."

The Chemistry Exhibit!

The Noble Gases had probably gone back to their portion of the exhibit.

"Follow me Mitry."

Mitry followed Dr. Hathale through Biology and past the rocket ship in the Air & Space Exhibit to the Chemistry Exhibit.

Ms. Detore and Aiden were waiting for them at the wall with Noble Gases painted across the top.

Mitry ran past her teacher and her friend to run her fingers down the wall. Helium (HE), Neon (NE), Argon (AR), Krypton (KR), Xenon (XE), and Radon (RN). They were all listed there.

"Helium? Hello? Can you pop out of the wall?" There was no response.

Mitry sniffled. It looked like there were a few things she was going to miss about STEM-Land.

"I'm sorry I didn't get to say thank you or good-bye." She whispered.

"Wow, it sure is great to see someone this excited about elements." remarked Ms. Detore. "Spending time in your lab must of had an effect on her."

Dr. Hathale smiled. "I hope so! Although we only know about the Noble Gases, we suspect that there are more elements out there. We need young scientists like Mitry and the rest of your students to discover and research them."

Mitry turned away from the wall.

"What do you mean, we only know about the Noble Gases?" she asked.

"What about Aluminum or Tin? They're part of the post-transition metals on the periodic table."

Ms. Detore and Dr. Hathale looked at Mitry with concern.

"What about the Halogens? The Metalloids?" continued Mitry.

"I've studied elements my whole life and I've never heard of those elemental families." said Dr. Hathale.

Mitry looked at her teacher and Dr. Hathale with suspicion. This was a very odd prank.

"I'll show you." said Mitry with determination. She marched over to where the Halogen exhibit should have been but the wall was blank except for a large black question mark.

The Metalloid wall was the same.

"This, this isn't possible!" Mitry protested.

She turned to face her best friend. "Aiden, don't you remember these walls were covered in information? We passed them on our way to the Noble Gases."

Aiden shook his head. His floppy black hair flicked from one side of his forehead to the other. He did not remember.

Mitry pulled up the Periodic Table of Elements on her smartwatch. She tapped it twice so that it appeared as a hologram floating above the watch screen. The entire table was blank except for the Noble Gases.

"That can't be right." She mumbled.

She searched for another periodic table, and another. All of the tables were blank except for the Noble Gases. The elements were missing!

How could that be? She remembered the periodic table from before her adventure. It had been full of elements! She'd even seen Aluminum and Tin in STEM-Land. She knew that they existed!

"Oh no!" she gasped.

What if Aluminum and Tin hadn't made it back with Mitry and the Noble Gases because they weren't on the target when Argon pressed the blue button to send them all home?

She thought back to her first conversation with AC and DC. They had said that she'd need to stand on the target when the blue button was pushed to go home. The Noble Gases were the only elements that had been on the target with her and now they were

67

the only elements that still existed in her world!

She looked at Ms. Detore, Dr. Hathale, and Aiden.

"I have to go back." She told them. "I have to bring back the rest of the elements from STEM-Land!"

"STEM-Land? Mitry, what are you talking about?" said Dr. Hathale.

Mitry patted the pockets of her lab coat looking for the remote. Where was that remote?

The museum lab!

She had to get to the remote before it got lost or thrown out.

Without another word Mitry took off running. She ran through the Chemistry Exhibit, past the rocket ship in the Air & Space Exhibit, through Biology and back to the door that read Staff Only.

Dr. Hathale, Ms. Detore, and Aiden chased after her. Aiden, the fastest of the three, pulled ahead of the adults. He was catching up to Mitry!

Mitry threw open the Staff Only door. There on the ground, beneath the empty periodic table poster, was the remote.

With Aiden on her heels, she sprinted toward the remote, scooped it up, and slammed her thumb down on the green button.

The End
(for now)

FACT PACK

from STEM-Land; The Noble Gases Come to the Rescue

The Noble Gases

The Noble Gases are the six elements in the far right hand column, Group 18, on the Periodic Table of Elements.

The Nobles Gases are colorless, odorless, tasteless and non-flammable gases. All of the Noble Gases have the maximum number of electrons that they can hold in their outer shell. This makes the Noble Gases very stable and unreactive (they don't combine easily with other elements).

Helium

Helium was first spotted by an astronomer, Jules Janssen, in 1868 during a solar eclipse. Months later, another astronomer, Norman Lockyer, and chemist Edward Franklin named the unknown element, Helium. The name Helium was derived from the Greek word for sun, helios, because at that point Helium had only been observed on the sun.

In 1882, a physicist, Luigi Palmieri spotted Helium on Earth for the first time when he was studying lava from Mt. Vesuvius.

As you learned in STEM-Land: The Noble Gases, Helium is a gas that is lighter than air. It's the reason helium balloons float! Helium is also used in party balloons, weather balloons, and blimps.

Argon, Krypton, Xenon and Neon

Chemist William Ramsay played a major role in discovering Argon, Krypton, Xenon and Neon. In 1894, Ramsay and physicist John Strutt discovered Argon. Four years later Ramsay and chemist Morris Travers discovered Krypton, Neon and Xenon.

In STEM-Land: The Noble Gases, Argon generates a lightbulb above his head whenever he gets a good idea. This is because in the real world, Argon is used in light bulbs. The light bulbs in your home may very well have Argon in them!

In the book, Krypton, Neon and Xenon also have traits related to their uses. Krypton is used in photographer's lights and medical lasers. Krypton uses both during the laser-light battle with the Magician, AC, and DC.

Neon uses signs to point out information throughout the book because in real life, Neon is often used in bright, glowing advertising signs.

Xenon is used in strobe lights. This comes in handy when Xenon is able to temporarily blind AC and DC when Mitry and the Noble Gases are trying to escape.

Radon

Radon was discovered in 1900 by physicist, Friedrich Ernst Dorn.

Chemists, Marie Curie and her husband, Pierre Curie, had noticed that when the element Radium was exposed to air, the air became radioactive. The Curies didn't know why this happened, and they didn't look into it but Dorn did.

When Dorn looked into what was happening he discovered that Radon gas was produced when Radium fell apart and that it was Radon that was making the air radioactive!

In STEM-Land: The Noble Gases, Radon wears a protective radiation suit under his noble clothes to protect everyone else from his radiation.

The Periodic Table of Elements

What is it?

The Periodic Table of Elements organizes chemical elements in a grid of rows and columns. On the Periodic Table the rows are called periods and columns are called groups. From left to right and top to bottom, the elements are listed in order by their atomic number.

Each element has its own square on the grid. The one or two letter abbreviation in each square is that element's symbol. The symbols make it easier for people to write chemical formulas and equations.

There are two numbers within the square. The number in the top right corner is that element's atomic number. The atomic number is the number of protons in each atom of that element.

The number at the bottom of the square is that element's atomic weight. The atomic weight is the average mass of atoms that occur naturally in that element.

Dmitri Mendeleev

Dmitri Mendeleev, a Russian chemist and teacher, was one of many people to propose a way to organize the elements.

Mendeleev discovered that when he organized the known elements in columns by their atomic weight the elements within each row also shared similarities. This is called Periodic Law!

He based his Periodic Table of Elements on the principals of Periodic Law. This system of organization made it possible for Mendeleev to predict the existence of undiscovered elements and the properties they would have.

As the elements he predicted were discovered Mendeleev and his Periodic Table of Elements earned their place in history. He even earned his own element on the Periodic Table, Mendelevium (Md).

In STEM-Land: The Noble Gases, the main character Mitry Mendel's name was inspired by Dmitri Mendeleev.

Scientific Visitors to STEM-Land

Leonardo Da Vinci

Leonardo Da Vinci, born in 1452, was a famous Italian inventor, scientist, artist, and engineer from the Renaissance time period. Da Vinci believed that science and art were equally important as science could teach creative people how to produce better art and artistic creativity could improve scientific thinking.

He lived out his beliefs by contributing a wide range of inventions to the world among them flying machines, parachutes, submarines, swimming fins, swing bridges, street-lighting systems, contact lenses, as well as a wide range of arts including the Mona Lisa and The Last Supper.

Ada Lovelace

Ada Lovelace, born in 1815, was an English mathematician. She was tasked with translating an article about a new calculation machine. As she translated the article she also included her own thoughts on the machine's potential. She rightfully predicted that codes could be created to enable the machine to understand letters and symbols as well as numbers. She also predicted that it would be possible for the machine to repeat a series of instructions, a process known as looping that computer programs use today.

Although her contributions to the field of computer science until the 1950s, today, she is considered to be the world's first computer programmer. There's even a computer language, Ada, named in her honor!

Marie Daly

Marie Daly, born in 1921, was an American chemist. In 1947, she became the first African-American woman to receive a doctorate in chemistry in the United States.

She conducted important research on cholesterol, sugars, and proteins and helped discover the relationship between high cholesterol, clogged arteries and heart attacks. Her work helped improve society's understanding of how diet can affect the health of the heart and the circulatory system.

In addition to her research, Daly championed efforts to get students of color enrolled in medical schools and graduate science programs.

Science Experiments from STEM-Land; The Noble Gases Come to the Rescue

Elephant Toothpaste

What You'll Need:

A clean 16-oz plastic soda bottle
1/2 cup 20-volume hydrogen peroxide liquid (6% solution)
1 Tablespoon (one packet) of dry yeast
3 Tablespoons of warm water
Liquid dishwashing soap
Small cup
Safety goggles

Optional:

Food Coloring
Funnel for easier pouring

Instructions:

As you know from STEM-Land: The Noble Gases Come to the Rescue, foam will shoot out from the bottle, so be sure to do this experiment on a washable surface, or place the bottle on a tray or tarp.

Hydrogen peroxide can irritate skin and eyes, so put on those safety goggles and carefully pour the hydrogen peroxide into the bottle.
Add 8 drops of your favorite food coloring into the bottle.
Add 1 tablespoon of liquid dish soap into the bot-

Ashley McAlpin

tle and swish the bottle around a bit to mix it.

In a separate small cup, combine the warm water and yeast together and mix for 30 seconds.

Pour the yeast water mixture into the bottle (a funnel helps here) and get ready for the foam explosion!

What's Happening:

When you added the yeast to the bottle the yeast acted as a catalyst (a helper) to remove the oxygen from the hydrogen peroxide. Since it did this very fast, it created lots and lots of bubbles. All of those bubbles create the foam.

Did you notice the bottle got warm? Your experiment created a reaction called an **exothermic reaction**. An exothermic reaction is a chemical reaction that releases energy either by light or heat. In your experiment, the exothermic reaction releases energy by heat!

The Magician's Density Magic Trick

What You'll Need:

2 clear, equally sized glasses
vegetable oil (enough to fill the cups)
water (enough to fill the cups)
Index card
Food coloring
Measuring cup

Instructions:

Fill one glass with water and one glass with vegetable oil. Use the measuring cup to make sure you put an equal amount of water and vegetable oil into the respective glasses.

Add a few drops of your favorite food coloring into the water cup and mix until you are happy with the color. The food coloring will make it easier for you to tell the water and vegetable oil apart.

Place the index card over the top of the vegetable oil glass. Holding the index card in place, flip the glass of vegetable oil upside down and place it on top of the glass of water.

Slowly, slide the index card out from between the two glasses. Even without the index card dividing the two glasses, the liquids won't mix!

What's Happening?

As the Magician explained in STEM-Land: The Noble Gases the vegetable oil floats on top of the water because the vegetable oil is less dense than the water.

If you do the experiment in reverse, water on top of vegetable oil, you'll observe the water and vegetable oil switch sides as the water sinks to the bottom and the vegetable oil floats to the top.

Take it a step further:

Don't let the learning stop here! Get another tall, clear glass and slowly pour in the following liquids in the order below.

¼ c. honey
¼ c. corn syrup
¼ c. maple syrup
¼ c. milk
¼ c. water (dyed your favorite color)
¼ c. vegetable oil
¼ c. rubbing alcohol (dyed your favorite color with food coloring)

These liquids all have different densities so you'll end up with a glass full of defined, colorful layers. Before you start take a guess at which liquid you think is the densest.

Do the layers match up with what you expected?

The Magician's Water Knot Trick

What You'll Need:

1 empty 2-Liter Soda Bottle
1 nail
Scissor
Water (enough to fill the bottle)

Instructions:

Trim the top off the bottle, above the label. Peel off the label. Use the nail to poke several holes between 2-5 holes about 1/4-inch apart. Make sure they are not further apart than this.

Fill the bottle with water until it's almost full. Watch the water stream out the holes.

Run your fingers over the bottle's surface and pinch the water streams together (i.e. tying it in knots). Slide your hands across the holes again to separate them.

What's Happening?

Water molecules are attracted to each other and stick together, this causes the streams of water to "bond," seemingly tying the water streams in knots.

The Magician's Bending Water Trick

What You'll Need:

A plastic comb
Water (from a faucet or hose)
A head full of clean dry hair

Instructions:

Turn the tap on to make a steady stream of water.
Run a comb through your hair three times. It works best if your hair is dry and clean.

Put the comb near the water (but don't touch the water). Watch the water bend!

Run a comb through your hair again to repeat the experiment!

What's Happening?

Static electricity! Static electricity often happens when you rub things together (like when you rub your hands together very quickly) Combing your hair moves negatively charged electrons from your hair onto the comb. This makes the comb negatively charged.

When you bring the negatively charged comb near the water it is attracted to the positive charge of the water. The attraction is strong enough to actually pull the water towards the comb as it is bending!

The Magician's Water Disappearing Trick

What You'll Need:

1 ½ Sodium polyacrylate (available on Amazon)
A cup that you can't see through
Water (from a faucet or pitcher or bottle)
Measuring spoons
Measuring cups

Instructions:

Pour 1 tablespoon of sodium polyacrylate into the

bottom of the cup.
Pour 1/4 cup of water into the cup.
Wait for 1 minute.
Turn the cup over and try to pour the water out!

What's Happening?

Absorption! Sodium polyacrylate acts like a sponge and absorbs moisture. When mixed with water, it turns into a solid gel. Once it forms a gel, the water is no longer liquid and can't pour out. The particles in sodium polyacrylate are hygroscopic, which means that they absorb and hold water. This is why sodium polyacrylate is used in baby diapers! It absorbs moisture and keep babies dry and comfortable.

The Magician's Color Changing Flower Trick

What You'll Need:

A white flower (we recommend roses or carnations)
A vase
Water (from a faucet or pitcher or bottle)
Food coloring
Scissors

Instructions:

Fill the glass halfway with water.

Put 2-5 drops of food coloring (pick one color we recommend your favorite) into the water.

Trim half an inch of stem off the flower and then put it in the glass.

Wait overnight.

The next day you'll see that your flower has turned your favorite color!

What's Happening?

Capillary action! Capillary action is what flowers and other plants use to bring water up to the top of the plant where it is used to provide water and nutrients to every part of the plant. In this experiment, the water and the food coloring are both pulled up through the plant stem to feed the plant. This process is similar to how towels soak up water.

Take it a step further:

Don't let the magic stop here! Get another glass and another white flower. Cut the stem length-wise up to an inch below the flower head. Insert each half of the stem into a different colored water. Observe how the petals change color.

Mitry's Makerspace Black Light

What You'll Need:

A blue permanent marker

A purple permanent marker
Clear tape
Smartphone or tablet with LED flash
A yellow Highlighter
White paper

Instructions:

Place a small strip of tape over the LED flash on the back of your smartphone or tablet (it should be close to your rear camera).

Color the tape strip with blue marker so that it covers the flash.

Place another strip of tape over the first strip.

Color the second strip of tape with the blue marker.

Place a third and final strip of tape over the flash, but this time color it with the purple marker.

Take the yellow highlighter and draw a door on the white paper.

Turn off all the lights so that the room is dark and you can't see anything on the paper.

Turn on your smartphone/tablet's flashlight and shine it on the paper to reveal the Disappearing Door!

What's Happening?

Some highlighters use ink that contains fluorescent dyes. Fluorescence is a type of glow that is triggered by another form of energy, for example by light. The light waves from ultraviolet light (from the blacklight device) excites the molecules on the dye causing them to reflect back light.

About the Author

Ashley McAlpin loved all things science when she was growing up in Southern California, but as she got older she began to compare how "smart" she was to how "smart" she thought other people were. This caused her to decide too early in life that she didn't have the right "brain" for STEM.

As an adult, Ashley found herself working at an internationally known technology company. Surrounded by so many brilliant minds and innovative STEM inventions Ashley was inspired to revisit her first love, science, and to increase her own knowledge of STEM.

This time Ashley wasn't afraid about not being "smart," she knew that anything she didn't know she could learn. With this new attitude Ashley dove into learning more about science, technology, engineering, and math.

Eager to share her love for STEM, Ashley wrote a story STEM-Land; The Noble Gases Come to the Rescue. Many of the STEM activities mentioned in the book can be found on her website stem-land.com.

Ashley's goal is to encourage all people who may think they aren't "smart" enough for STEM to discover their inner scientist like she did.

Made in the USA
San Bernardino, CA
14 November 2019

59894302R00054